Diego's Birthday Surprise

by Lara Bergen
illustrated by Art Mawhinney

Ready-to-Read

Simon Spotlight/Nick Jr.
New York   London   Toronto   Sydney

Based on the TV series *Go, Diego, Go!*™ as seen on Nick Jr.®

SIMON SPOTLIGHT
An imprint of Simon & Schuster Children's Publishing Division
1230 Avenue of the Americas, New York, New York 10020

Manufactured in the United States of America
4 6 8 10 9 7 5 3
Library of Congress Cataloging-in-Publication Data
Bergen, Lara.
Diego's birthday surprise / by Lara Bergen ; illustrated by Art Mawhinney.
— 1st ed.
p. cm. — (Ready-to-read ; [level 1])
"Based on the TV series Go, Diego, Go! as seen on Nick Jr."
ISBN-13: 978-1-4169-5431-6
ISBN-10: 1-4169-5431-7
I. Mawhinney, Art. II. Go, Diego, go! (Television program) III. Title.
PZ7.B44985Dim 2008
2007027668

Hi! My name is 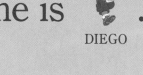.

This is .

Do you know what today is?

It is  's birthday!

BABY JAGUAR

We will have a party.

It will be a surprise party!

has a of all of the

ALICIA   LIST

things we need.

First on the list is .
CHORIZO

 is a special treat
CHORIZO

for .
BABY JAGUAR

He loves to eat meat.

What else is on the ?
We need party , ,
HATS PRESENTS
and .
BALLOONS

PARTY LIST
Chorizo
Party hats
Presents
Balloons

We have 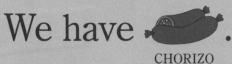.

CHORIZO

We have party snacks for everyone!

We have party .

HATS

We have  .

PRESENTS

But where are the 🎈 ?

BALLOONS

HAP

Look out the !
WINDOW

The  have the !

BOBOS   BALLOONS

Say "Freeze, !"

BOBOS

Oops!

The  **BOBOS** let the

BALLOONS go!

They are sorry.

Hurry! We have to get the  back! BALLOONS

BABY JAGUAR will be at

the ANIMAL RESCUE CENTER soon!

 can help us find the  .

CLICK

BALLOONS

Just say "  !"

CLICK

CLICK

RAINFOREST

will zoom through the

to look for the

BALLOONS

Are these  ?

BALLOONS

No, those are .

FLOWERS

Are these  ?

BALLOONS

Yes!

The **BALLOONS** are up in the **TREE**.

RESCUE PACK can help us

get up the **TREE** to the **BALLOONS**.

Can we use a  to

KAYAK

reach the top of the 🌳 ?

TREE

No.

Can we climb a 🪜 to

LADDER

reach the top of the 🌳 ?

TREE

Yes!

Hooray!

We did it!

We got the 🎈 !

BALLOONS

Look! It is .

We need to hurry.

 is coming!

Let's go!

We have to get the  BALLOONS

back to the ANIMAL RESCUE CENTER

fast.

Yeah!

We made it just in time.

Surprise!

Happy birthday,  !

BABY JAGUAR